# BOOK REVIEWS

Here's what people are saying:

A pleasing bedtime story . . .
from SCHOOL LIBRARY JOURNAL

. . . illustrations that play up the
inherent silliness . . . For the bedtime
story repertoire.
from BOOKLIST

Richly hued paintings of the
anthropomorphs burst with life, humor
and imaginative touches . . .
from PUBLISHERS WEEKLY

Weekly Reader Children's Book Club presents

MOTHER, MOTHER, I WANT ANOTHER

by Maria Polushkin
illustrated by Diane Dawson

CROWN PUBLISHERS, INC.
New York

Text copyright © 1978 by Maria Polushkin
Illustrations copyright © 1978 by Diane Dawson
All rights reserved. No part of this publication may be reproduced, stored in a retrieval system, or transmitted, in any form or by any means, electronic, mechanical, photocopying, recording, or otherwise, without prior written permission of the publisher. Inquiries should be addressed to Crown Publishers, Inc., One Park Avenue, New York, N.Y. 10016. Manufactured in the United States of America. Published simultaneously in Canada by General Publishing Company Limited.

The text of this book is set in 18 point Garamond. The illustrations are line drawings, with half-tone overlays, prepared by the artist, for blue, red, and yellow.

Library of Congress Cataloging in Publication Data
Polushkin, Maria.   Mother, Mother, I want another.
Summary: Anxious to get her son to sleep, Mrs. Mouse goes off to find what she thinks he wants. [1. Mice—Fiction. 2. Sleep—Fiction] I. Dawson, Diane. II. Title. PZ7.P7695Mo
[E]   78-5443   ISBN 0-517-53401-0

To Robin

It was bedtime in the mouse house.
Mrs. Mouse took baby mouse to his room.

She helped him put
on his pajamas

and told him
to brush his teeth.

She tucked him
into his bed

and read him
a bedtime story.

She gave him a bedtime kiss,
and then she said, "Good night."

But as she was leaving,
baby mouse started to cry.
"Why are you crying?" asked Mrs. Mouse.

"I want another, Mother."

"Another mother!" cried
Mrs. Mouse. "Where will I find
another mother for my baby?"

Mrs. Mouse ran to get Mrs. Duck.
"Please, Mrs. Duck, come to our house and help put
baby mouse to bed. Tonight he wants another mother."

Mrs. Duck came and sang a song:

Quack, quack, mousie,
Don't you fret.
I'll bring you worms
Both fat and wet.

But baby mouse said,
"Mother, Mother, I want another."

Mrs. Duck went to get Mrs. Frog.

Mrs. Frog came and sang:

Croak, croak, mousie,
Close your eyes.
I will bring you
Big fat flies.

But baby mouse said,
"Mother, Mother, I want another."

Mrs. Frog went to get Mrs. Pig.

Mrs. Pig came and sang a song:

Oink, oink, mousie,
Go to sleep.
I'll bring some carrots
For you to keep.

But baby mouse said,
"Mother, Mother, I want another."

Mrs. Pig went to get Mrs. Donkey.

Mrs. Donkey came and sang a song:

Hee-haw, mousie,
Hush-a-bye.
I'll sing for you
A lullaby.

But baby mouse
had had enough.

"NO MORE MOTHERS!"
he shouted.

"I want another
KISS."

"Well, now!"

"Really?"

Mrs. Duck
kissed baby mouse.

Mrs. Frog kissed
baby mouse.

Mrs. Pig kissed
baby mouse.

And Mrs. Donkey
kissed baby mouse.

Then Mrs. Mouse gave baby mouse a drink
of water. She tucked in his blanket.

And she gave
him a kiss.

Baby mouse smiled.
"May I have another, Mother?"

"Of course," said Mrs. Mouse, and she
leaned over and gave him *another* kiss.